PASSING FOR WHITE

First published in 2017 in Great Britain by
Barrington Stoke Ltd
18 Walker Street, Edinburgh, EH3 7LP

www.barringtonstoke.co.uk

Text © 2017 Tanya Landman

A CIP catalogue record for this book is available
from the British Library upon request

ISBN: 978-1-78112-681-3

Printed in China by Leo

TANYA LANDMAN

PASSING FOR WHITE

Barrington Stoke

To Reginald D Hunter.
Thanks for the 53%

"I had much rather starve in England, a free woman, than be a slave for the best man that ever breathed upon the American continent."

Ellen Craft

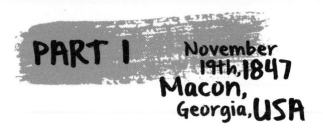

Benjamin

She was standing on the step.

Scaring me to death.

A white woman.

Talking nice. Acting polite.

Looking at me.

Looking at me, straight in the eye.

Looking at me, straight in the eye and smiling.

What in the name of God was going on?

The Cornwells were new in town. Husband and wife had taken the big house on the corner by the church. I'd been sent along to measure up for new cabinets and shelves – there was a whole heap of work to do. My master told me their girl would show me the rooms.

"Rosa," he said. "She's called Rosa. That's who you got to ask for, boy."

I went to the back door. Knocked. When it opened, I was expecting to see a slave.

So I looked her full in the face. She sure was a beautiful thing, tall, with straight black hair. Brown eyes. White skin.

White skin. White skin. White, white, white. Hellfire!

Not Rosa. No slave. She was the lady of the house! Oh Lord! And I was looking right at her! A man like me could get himself killed for less than that.

I dropped my head, my heart bang, bang, banging against my ribs. I felt sick to the stomach.

"You must be Benjamin," she said. Polite. Warm. I could feel her smile burning into the top of my head. "Won't you come on in?"

I was expecting her to call the girl, Rosa, but maybe she was running errands. It was just the two of us.

She led and I followed. We went down along the corridor to the parlour, where she pointed to the fireplace.

"Right there," she said. "Mr Cornwell wants two cabinets about so high, either side. And shelves just here. Think you can manage that?"

"Yes, ma'am."

My mind was pumping like a steam train. I'd seen ladies like her before. They acted kind. Generous. But put a foot wrong and they'd be calling for a whipping. Heck! It didn't have to be a foot wrong. It could be a toe. A toenail. The hair on a big toe. Not even that.

Sometimes, you didn't know what set them off. They'd go at you for no reason at all.

White folks could do whatever the hell they pleased. I knew that. And then they'd say it was your own damned fault. They'd lie so well they'd have themselves believing it. I was praying for that woman to go away. Thinking, 'Get out of here. Go someplace else. Leave me alone to do my work.'

But she stayed to watch me. And out of the corner of my eye I could see she was smiling again.

Then she started talking.

I couldn't make any sense of it. I was too darned scared.

I was on my own in a room with a white woman. One word of hers could kill me.

My hands were shaking. When I got out my tape measure I dropped it. I had it wound into a ball and it rolled across the floor. Stopped right at her feet.

"Here, let me." She picked it up. Came on over. Held it out for me to take.

I froze. Couldn't move a muscle.

So she reached out. Took my hand in one of hers.

Her white palm cupping the back of my hand. Giving me the tape measure, the tips of her white fingers brushing my brown skin. Standing so close I could smell her sweet breath.

And her touch did something to me. I was feeling all those things you're not supposed to feel. All those things you're not allowed to feel.

"There you go," she said.

Then she was smiling again.

Talking. Chattering. The words didn't make any more sense than birds screeching.

What the devil was she doing? Playing with me? Testing me? Trying me out? Was this some kind of trap?

I wanted to get away! My heart was thumping so hard I thought my ribs would crack.

Then I heard a creak of floorboards upstairs. A voice called, "Rosa? Where are you?"

And the woman whose hands had touched mine was saying, "I'm down in the parlour, Miss Abigail. The boy's here about the cabinets like Mr Cornwell said."

"Well, come up here." The upstairs voice whined. "My hair needs fixing."

She turned to go. But before she did I said, "Rosa? You're Rosa? The house girl?"

"Yes." She was already on her way out of the door. But she looked back at me. "Who'd you think I was?"

I couldn't reply. She was already running up the stairs.

To Miss Abigail.

Her mistress? Her owner?

Everything flipped on its head.

Rosa.

She may have looked white. But to them?

That woman was as black as me.

Rosa

It wasn't the first time I'd been taken for white. I was taken for white so often that I got given away.

My old mistress was sick to death of folks thinking I was her child. So when her eldest daughter – Miss Abigail – got married I was one of the wedding presents.

I was eleven years old at the time.

Slaves get bought. Slaves get sold. Slaves get handed over as gifts. There doesn't have to be a special reason for it but in my case, there was.

My old master was also my daddy. No one said it. Not aloud. But everyone knew it, including his wife. My skin was almost as pale as his. I had his eyes. His nose. His chin.

My mother was a slave, so I was his property too. But my looks were a daily reminder to his wife of the things he did when she wasn't watching. I was a constant source of shame, so when she had the opportunity to get rid of me she took it.

Parting from my mother was the most pain I'd ever felt. The most pain I ever hoped to feel. We knew we wouldn't see each other again. Not in this world.

You'd think grief like that would tear you apart. Make you scream and cry. Make you howl and roar.

But it doesn't.

It makes you cold. Makes your heart into a lump of stone inside you. Makes your arms and legs feel so heavy they might be filled with lead.

The day I left, I shut down. As I rode along on the top of a cart that followed the newly-weds' carriage, I was like a house whose owner had died. Windows boarded up, doors bolted. No fire in the grate, no lamps burning, nothing cooking on the stove. Every feeling I had was covered over with dust sheets. I was cold. Dark. Empty.

Time passed. I grew up.

Then, one fine morning when I'd just turned seventeen, I opened the door of Miss Abigail's house and saw Benjamin Carter on the step.

For the first time in six years I felt my heart start beating.

I didn't realise he'd taken me for white. I thought he just didn't like me. Maybe I was making a fool of myself, talking and smiling like that, but I couldn't help it. When Miss Abigail called me up to fix her hair it was a relief. I kept thinking – calm down. Get a hold of yourself, girl. Stop behaving like a crazy fool, child.

Then I went back down the stairs.

And he grinned at me and my insides were flip-flapping all over the place.

"How about we start on over?" he said. He cleared his throat. Stood up straight. Looked me in the eye. "Miss Rosa, my name's Benjamin. It's a real pleasure to make your acquaintance, ma'am." He gave a little bow just like white folks do. There was a teasing look on his face that made me smile. I dropped him a curtsey.

"Why thank you, kind sir."

He held his hand out. I took it. My palm rested in his. A perfect fit. That was that.

My heart was snagged, like a fish on a line. I was hooked. Landed, high and dry.

Gasping for breath. Helpless.

Rosa

Falling in love isn't a good idea, not if you're a slave. Feeling anything at all just gets you hurt. But by the time Benjamin finished all the work Mr Cornwell wanted doing on the house, he and I were both in so deep there was no getting out again.

I'd sworn when I was eleven years old that I was never going to marry or have children. I'd seen my mother's heart torn apart – I didn't want to feel that too. But there was no resisting Benjamin. And we were lucky, I guess. He went to his master and his master spoke to mine and, after a little horse trading between the two of them, they said we could marry.

When I heard that news? It should have been a joyful day. But when Miss Abigail called me in to tell me, her husband was in the room standing right behind her. She couldn't see the look on his face, but I could. That light in his eyes ... bright, like there was a candle burning inside his skull. The way he ran his tongue across his lips twisted a knife in my guts.

It isn't an easy thing to confess to. But it has to be done.

Leaving my mother wasn't the only thing that had turned me dead and cold inside. Leaving my mother was just the start of it.

Miss Abigail was a lady. And like all Southern ladies, she didn't know diddly squat about men. She thought 'love' was all romance – dancing and flirting and swooning. My mistress hadn't so much as kissed her husband before she married him. How babies were made was a mystery to her.

The morning after her wedding she was shaking like a leaf. I thought her eyes were going to pop out across the breakfast table. She'd found out that there were things a husband expected of a wife. And the things he loved to do were things that she hated.

It might have amused me. If things had turned out different maybe I'd have split my sides laughing. But it wasn't long before he took to slipping into my room in the middle of the night.

I was a child. Heck! I was her sister!

But Miss Abigail turned a blind eye. And I was her slave. There wasn't anything I could say or anything I could do about any of it.

Rosa

It's possible to cut your mind right down the middle. Two halves. Two lives. Each one quite separate from the other.

What the master did to me, and what Benjamin and I did to each other when we were alone – it was like those things were done by two completely different women.

My two lives stayed apart for months. And then they came slamming together, and collided with an impact so hard everything shattered into pieces.

One morning, I got up and knew I was carrying a child.

Now, I've met women who had no idea a baby was growing inside of them until that baby started trying to get itself out. But me? I felt different the moment I opened my eyes.   It's hard to explain. I just knew. And nothing could have been worse.

See, up until the day I married Benjamin, Mr Cornwell had been careful not to get a child on me. Miss Abigail might pretend she couldn't hear the creaking of my bed, but if my belly started to swell – well, then there would be some explaining to do, wouldn't there?

Then Benjamin came along and we got permission to wed. And after I was married? There was no stopping my master. He could do whatever he liked. That's why his eyes had lit up that day. If a baby took root in my belly he could pass it off as Benjamin's.

But I loved my husband too much to do that to him.

Rosa

I hadn't lied to Benjamin. But I hadn't told him the truth either. I'd shut that away in my head. Locked and bolted it inside a dark room. Thrown away the key. I couldn't admit to myself what the master was doing to me, so how could I find the words to tell Benjamin? But the baby growing inside of me forced that door open. Light leaked in and I couldn't go on ignoring it.

It was two weeks before I could see my husband. I was married to him, but Miss Abigail had me waiting on her hand and foot all her waking hours. And night times ... well. I already said about the night times.

I was unusual having a room all to myself. Benjamin had to bed down on the floor of his master's workshop. Any time I was allowed to see him, that's where I slept too.

When I told him I was expecting, we were sitting on a blanket in the sawdust, with a tallow lamp burning on the floor. The joy on his face just about killed me. But I couldn't let him go on thinking what he was thinking.

"It isn't ours, Benjamin."

He didn't understand what I was saying. He took my hand in his. "Sugar, I know that. But they've been kind to us so far, haven't they? They surely won't go selling our child, not if we tread careful."

"No, Benjamin, I don't mean that," I said. "I mean – I can't be sure it's yours."

There was a silence. I could hear my husband's breathing. The blood pumping in my ears. The turning of his thoughts.

"Not mine?" he said slowly. "What do you mean?"

It was like spitting cut glass from my throat. "I don't know if you're the daddy."

"Who then?"

"Master."

I couldn't say any more. Couldn't look at him. Couldn't bear to see the pain in his eyes. Didn't want to watch his face change from love to loathing. I was hurting so much I curled into a ball. Once I'd started crying I couldn't stop. I was trying to tell him 'sorry', but what came out was an unholy kind of noise.

I could feel him raging. The anger and the sorrow was tearing through him like a storm. It was balling itself up in his chest. Any moment soon it would reach his fists.

I'd seen men who had to stand by and let their masters rape their women. Their wives. Their daughters, sisters, mothers. There was nothing anybody could do. And because no man could fight his master, his rage would turn on the woman he couldn't protect.

I was waiting for the blows to come raining down, thinking that if he killed me – if I died right here, right now, with the baby inside me – that would be an end to it. And I'd have welcomed it as a mercy.

But Benjamin didn't raise a hand against me. He hit the wall. Hit it so hard the skin of his knuckles split open. Blood was smeared across it. Then his arms were around me, so gentle, so tender, so strong. He was soothing me, rocking me like I was a child. Rocking us both. His tears were rolling down his face into my hair.

"There, hush now. Don't take on," he murmured. "It will be all right. It will. I'll make it all right."

"I'm so ashamed."

"The shame isn't yours, sugar," he told me. "It's theirs. It's his. We just got to find a way of bearing it."

We were holding each other like that for a long time. Rocking. Soothing. Clinging tight to the only good thing in both our lives.

When I did look in his face I could see that something in him had changed. There was a hardness that hadn't been there before. He whispered so low I could barely hear the words.

"Rosa, we've got to run."

"What?"

"It's time. I've been thinking of it a while now," he said. "Can't go delaying it any longer. I don't know how we can do it. It might kill us both. But dying's got to be better than living like this. We got to get ourselves free."

Freedom.

Oh, I'd thought of it before now. Of course I had. There wasn't a slave born who didn't dream of being free.

But I'd seen slave hunts. And there's nothing like the sight of a pack of dogs tearing a man apart to put you off the idea of running. Nothing like knowing what a gang of slave catchers do to a woman to make you want to keep your head down and stay put. My spirit had been broken. I was beaten.

Until now.

I hadn't had anyone to run with before.

The two halves of my life had come together. I couldn't carry on. Neither could Benjamin. Because this would be how it was – on and on and on – until the day we died. It didn't matter diddly squat that Benjamin and I were married. Child or no child, husband or no husband, Mr Cornwell would make free with me whenever he chose.

But now it wasn't just about me and Benjamin. I knew that the child I was carrying – whoever his daddy was – would be a slave like me and my mother before me. This child wouldn't be mine to love, to protect, to look after. My baby was livestock. Goods the master might sell any time he wanted.

The chances of us getting out alive were so thin they could have slipped like a coin down a crack in the floorboards. But I figured God had put this love in both our hearts for a reason. He must have meant for us to do something about it.

If we ran, God would be watching over us.

Wouldn't he?

December 15th, 1848
Dawn

Rosa

I'd spent my life listening to the whisperings that ran along the grapevine. Every slave in Georgia knew there were trains that could carry you to the ocean. Every slave in Georgia knew there were steamers that sailed from the coastal ports to the city of Philadelphia in the state of Pennsylvania, where runaways could walk free. From Philadelphia you could go on to Canada. Canada was part of the British Empire and slavery had been outlawed there when I was around four years old.

The journey was easy as pie – if you were white. But slaves couldn't travel unless they were with a master. We wouldn't even get out of town.

Macon was a thousand miles from Philadelphia. Benjamin and I talked and talked around in circles, talked until our tongues were worn out, talked ourselves ragged. By the end of it my eyes were drooping, Benjamin was yawning and we were neither of us any further on. We both caught some sleep, but I woke at dawn and lay there in the half-light looking at his face, thinking about that first time we met. How I'd put his tape measure back in his hand and scared him half to death because he'd taken me for white.

The ghost of an idea rose from my head. It hovered there in the air in front of me.

Maybe, just maybe, the thing that had got me given away might save the both of us.

I could pass for white. Suppose I did? Right out in the open? Miss Abigail gave me her worn-out dresses sometimes. That's why Benjamin had mistaken me for the lady of the house. If I pretended to be a white woman, if Benjamin was my slave ...?

But no – that would never work. A lady, travelling on her own with a valet, not a maid? That just wasn't right. It would get us noticed. Questions would be asked.

I sighed with frustration. Someone like Mr Cornwell could go anywhere and no one even looked twice!

Oh.

What if ...? Just suppose ...?

I slipped out from under Benjamin's arm. Stood up. Took his trousers and stepped into them. Picked up his shirt. His jacket. Put them on. Then his hat.

Benjamin was stirring. His eyelids were fluttering. He was feeling across the blanket for me.

I cleared my throat, spoke to him the way I'd heard his master talk. "Hey, boy. Get up. There's work to be done."

His eyes flipped open. When he saw me standing over him, he almost leaped out of his skin. He reached for his clothes – which weren't there. I couldn't help but laugh.

"Rosa?" he said. "Rosa? What in the devil's name are you playing at?"

I couldn't speak for laughing and there's something about that noise that catches on like a disease.

Benjamin started to chuckle too, all the time protesting. "It isn't funny, Rosa. Heck, sugar, you frightened the life out of me."

He was hugging me tight. We were both crying with laughter, but then all of a sudden he stopped. He pushed me back, and held me at arm's length. Looked at me hard. He stared at my clothes. I knew he was thinking the same as me. For a moment he'd thought I was a white man. And if I could fool my own husband, maybe, just maybe, I could fool everyone else too.

Rosa

It seemed that God was truly smiling on us.

After that night with Benjamin I went back to Miss Abigail's. I found her sitting at the breakfast table with a letter in her hand and a frown on her face. Christmas was coming up and her mother had written to her to say she was coming to visit for the season.

Now I knew that some owners gave their slaves a few days off at Christmas time, but I'd never been on the receiving end of that kind of generosity. Christmas had always meant parties and dinners. There were new dresses to be sewn and hair to be fixed and shawls to be fetched and carried. Christmas always meant a whole heap of extra work for me and the rest of the house slaves.

I don't know what was in that letter, but I'm guessing Miss Abigail's mother had written something about not wanting me around. Miss Abigail's forehead was scrunched into lines with the effort of thinking. Then she said, "How'd you like a pass, Rosa? You could go see Benjamin for a few days. Spend Christmas with him." She looked at her husband. "Wouldn't that be the best thing?"

Mr Cornwell didn't look none too pleased. But with his mother-in-law in the house he couldn't go creeping along the corridor to me at night. He glanced at his wife, stared at me, nodded, and that was that.

I stood there trying not to show on my face what I was feeling in my heart. A fearful thrill was running through me. My mouth was dry, the rest of me sheened with sweat. My mind was racing with plans. What if Benjamin could get a pass from his master too? Why then we'd have five days at Christmas. If God was willing, that would be five days when no one would come looking for either of us.

Five days when we could be running for our lives.

PART 2

Rosa

Benjamin's master fussed and fumed and cussed but – as masters go – he was one of the more obliging kind. He wrote out a pass.

My husband told his master he'd be spending the five days with me. I told mine I'd be with Benjamin. Just as long as our owners didn't meet and get to talking about us – and why would they? – we had five clear days. Days that might never come our way again.

When the morning came to leave I felt sick to the stomach. Whether it was terror of what was coming, or the baby growing inside me was hard to tell. I guess maybe it was both.

I left my master's home in broad daylight with his written permission clutched tight in my hand. If

I looked a little more rounded than I had before,
if I walked a little slower and with a little more
care? Well, Miss Abigail put that down to the fact
that I was with child. Neither she nor her husband
suspected I had a set of gentleman's clothes bundled
up and hidden under my skirts.

Over the years Benjamin had been allowed to
take on extra carpentry work and he got to keep
a little of the money people paid for that. As for
me, well, there were times that Mr Cornwell's
conscience bothered him some. He'd slip me a
few coins, tell me to get myself 'something pretty'.
But I had no need of ribbons or frills. I put every
last cent in a jar, and so Benjamin and I both had
savings. In the last few days my husband had
started to spend them. It was against the law to sell
anything to a slave without his master's permission,
but there were places that turned a blind eye to
that. They'd charge twice the price for goods that
were half the quality, but they'd do it.

Piece by piece, from different traders all over
town, Benjamin had bought the clothes and I'd
stowed them away in the chest in my room. A
shirt. A coat. A neckerchief. The trousers were Mr
Cornwell's – an old pair that needed mending. Miss
Abigail had said he'd have to wait for them until
after Christmas because she'd needed a new dress

before her mother arrived. Benjamin was bringing me a hat and boots.

We met in the old barn just outside of town. Benjamin cut my hair down close against my head. I took off my woman's clothes, stowed them in the trunk he'd brought along and changed myself into a man.

"How do I look?" I asked him.

"You look fine. You feel all right?"

"No. You?"

"Sick as a dog."

He smiled. I tried to. It felt as if my face might crack. We both knew that the moment we left that barn, there was no going back. If we got caught we wouldn't be returned to the places we'd had before. No one ever kept a runaway. First, we'd be punished. If we survived that – and there was no saying we would – we'd get sold. And if we got sold, I wouldn't be a maid any more, and Benjamin wouldn't be a carpenter. We'd be separated. Sent to the cotton fields. If the punishment didn't kill us, the work surely would.

There was still time to forget this crazy plan. We could stay put. Get on with living. Make the best of what we had.

"You want to change your mind?" Benjamin said.

"No. You?"

"No."

"Let's get me bandaged up. Then we can be on our way."

I was plenty tall enough to carry off being a man. From a distance or in the dark I could pass, no problem. But we both knew full well that the moment anyone got close it would be obvious I was a woman. My skin was too soft, my chin too smooth, not even a trace of a shadow of stubble.

How to get around that had stumped the both of us until I remembered a friend of my old master's. Mr Stone used to scare the devil out me when I was a child. He got the rheumatics real bad. There were times they had to wrap him from the head down with hot towels to stop his joints from hurting. He sat out on the porch looking like a corpse wrapped in a winding sheet. You could smell the stinking liniment that the towels were soaked in right the way down the street.

That memory of Mr Stone had given me the idea that I'd be better to travel not as a healthy young man, but as an invalid. My face would be wrapped in bandages, my arm in a sling and my leg dragging behind me in a limp.

When I was ready, we walked back into town. I was leaning on a stick. My valet followed three steps behind, carrying the trunk that held my woman's clothes. We were heading for the train that would get us out of here. I'd been raised as a maid. I'd spent my life in bedrooms and parlours and dining rooms listening to white folks' talk. I could copy their tone, ape their manner, use their words. But it took every scrap of courage I possessed to walk up to that ticket office and pay the fares to Savannah for me and my slave.

But I did it. And after that – on the platform – Benjamin and I went our separate ways.

He stowed the trunk and went to sit in the negro carriage. I had to go sit with the white folks.

I was in disguise. Benjamin wasn't. I could only pray to God that no one on that platform would recognise him. Half the town seemed to be there. There were bound to be clients of Benjamin's master. Folks Benjamin had made things for. Chests. Tables. Chairs. People whose homes he'd been in.

But I told myself that so long as he kept his head down he'd be invisible. White folks don't look at black ones. And if they do, they can't hardly tell us apart. No one would give him a second glance.

But me? I was the opposite of invisible.

I was a stranger in town and that gave people reason enough to stare. On top of that I was an invalid. An oddity. Everyone – and I mean everyone – was looking my way, nudging each other. It made me break out into a sweat. As I climbed onto that train I guess I looked as sick as

I felt because I was helped along, helped to find a seat, helped to sit down. Told to make myself comfortable. Sure was strange having white folks talk to me so nice. Before long I was settled in a train carriage surrounded by white men. I remember thinking that there were a million and one ways our plan could all go wrong. And right from the start, it did.

Another man came in and plumped himself down in the seat across from me. I nearly died right there and then. It was a friend of my master's. He'd eaten dinner with the Cornwells only the week before. I'd been waiting on the table and this gentleman had an eye for a pale-skinned slave girl. He'd stared at my breasts all the time he was eating. And when the ladies left the room he made comments about me to my master that aren't fit to be repeated.

But my face was covered now. My hair was cut. I was in a gentleman's clothes in a white train carriage. I turned my face to the side and looked out of the window, trying to still the thumping of my heart.

The trouble with Southern folks is that they're so darned friendly. They like to talk. The train hadn't even left the station when people started asking each other where they were from and where they were headed.

Out of the corner of my eye I saw the man across from me nod me a greeting and heard him say, "Fine morning."

I froze. Turned to stone. I couldn't respond. Couldn't react at all. I kept looking out of the window.

He didn't like being ignored.

"Fine morning," he said again, a bit louder.

Still, I didn't react. I didn't know how to. My throat was so tight I couldn't have squeezed any words out, not even a "Yes". One of the other passengers laughed and it riled him even more.

"I said it's a fine morning, sir," he said even louder. "Can't you hear me?"

Can't you hear me?

It was like God was whispering in my ear. Suppose you can't hear? Why not play deaf?

So I carried right on ignoring him. He gave it one last try. Laying a hand on my arm so I couldn't fail to notice, he looked right into my face and said very slow and very loud, "Fine morning, sir."

I fixed my eyes on his mouth, frowned, as if I was reading his lips. Then I smiled a small smile. Nodded. Didn't say a word.

Now he was satisfied. He leaned back in his seat. The passenger who'd laughed said, "Sad affliction, to be deaf."

"Indeed. Well, I won't trouble him any more."

After that I sat there undisturbed, listening to their talk. I knew darned well that there were only three topics of conversation for the gentlemen of the South.

The price of cotton.

Troublesome, lazy negroes.

Those god-damned crazy abolitionists who wanted to free the slaves.

The length of that long, long train ride I heard plenty about all three. And I learned me a whole heap of cuss words too.

It was 200 long miles to Savannah. We arrived in the evening and the gentlemen who'd been in the carriage with me all went their separate ways. As soon as they were out of sight, the good Lord sent a miracle and I recovered both my hearing and my powers of speech.

Benjamin and I boarded an omnibus that carried us to the dock and from there we got on the steamer bound for Charleston. As soon as he helped me inside my cabin and closed the door behind us we collided. We clutched hold of each other, heads pressed together, whispering, "You all right?"

"Yes. You?"

"I'm fine. Fine."

Murmuring lies to comfort each other while our trembling bodies told the truth. We could have stayed like that the whole night through.

But, like I say, folks are friendly in the South. And a gentleman, keeping to himself? Staying all alone, in his cabin? With a slave?

I could hear the sound of eyebrows being raised on the other side of the cabin wall. With each heartbeat they got higher. We couldn't go drawing attention to ourselves, but I was worn out with the company of white gentlemen. I just didn't have the strength to go sit and listen to any more of them.

I blessed Mr Stone and his rheumatics then. Benjamin had bought a liniment in Macon. We hadn't used it on the train because it stank to high heaven.

But now it was time to make a big show of me being an invalid.

Benjamin took the flannels from my cabin to the gentlemen's saloon and warmed them on the stove. When they were done he soaked them with the liniment. The men sitting there supping whiskey were none too pleased to have their saloon filled with that stench, but it sure made the point that Benjamin's master was a truly sick man.

When Benjamin brought the flannels back, we had ourselves a little time alone. Time when no one's eyes were on us. Time when we could cling tight, soothe each other down.

He was supposed to be changing my old bandages for the warmed ones. When at last he did, they were all stone cold.

Benjamin couldn't stay the night in the cabin with me. After an hour or so he had to go back out on deck and find a place to sleep.

I was tucked up in that bunk but I can't say I slept much. Yet I knew it was worse for Benjamin.

On that steamer there was no place for slaves to rest. My husband spent the night perched on a pile of cotton sacks, huddled up by the funnel trying to keep warm. When he came back to me at first light, he looked sicker than I did.

Rosa

Come the morning, I was invited to eat at the Captain's table. Me, and half a dozen other men.

The Captain was asking my plans, and I was answering. The story Benjamin and I had agreed on was that I was heading north to see a doctor – an expert in treating the rheumatic condition I suffered so badly from.

The stinking liniment I'd been breathing in all night had affected my voice. It was coming out very low and very hoarse, but I was doing just fine. My arm was in a sling so Benjamin had to cut up my food for me. And it was then that I made a big mistake.

Once he'd sliced everything into small pieces, I dismissed him by saying, "Thank you, Benjamin."

I knew I'd done something wrong the moment the words left my mouth. There was a sudden chill in the air, and the eyes of all the men at the table swivelled in my direction. They looked at me. Then they looked at the Captain.

He cleared his throat. "You've a good boy there, sir. Quiet. Quick. Attentive. I like that. But you're a deal too kind to him."

Benjamin had retreated to the far corner in case I needed him again. He was standing, waiting with his head down. I couldn't help but look over.

I didn't reply to the Captain. I didn't have to. Another of the men at the table jumped in.

He was the kind of smooth-talking young Southern gentleman that women swooned over and men went drinking and gambling and whoring with. It seemed he'd decided I needed the benefit of his almighty wisdom.

"Look here," he said, his tone warm and friendly. He leaned towards me and I could smell last night's whiskey and cigar smoke on his breath. "Piece of advice for you. Never go thanking a slave for doing his duty."

Another of the men said, "Give them just one inch and they will take a mile."

And then they were all at it. All talking at once. A pack of hounds, seeing who could bark loudest.

"You've got to make them jump," Whiskey Breath said.

"You've got to keep them in their place."

"The harder you kick them, the better they serve."

"It does no good, being civil."

"You're storing up trouble there."

The Captain's voice rose over the baying of the pack. "You're planning on taking him north, you say?"

"I am, sir," I replied.

There was a chorus of disapproval. Sighs. Sucking of teeth. Shaking of heads.

Again, it was the Captain who said what they were all thinking. "You watch him like a hawk, you hear me? You think you've got yourself a good boy there but I've seen slaves change the moment they set foot on northern soil. They get a whiff of that air and it turns their heads."

There was only one man who hadn't said a word. He was no gentleman. White trash to the core, he was holding a leg of chicken in his fingers and had taken a big bite. When he spoke his words came out with a mess of chewed up flesh. I'm not repeating most of what he said. It wasn't fit for anyone's ears.

"You're right, Captain," White Trash said and a stream of cuss words followed. He looked hard at me. "If you take that nigger north, he'll run, and you won't be able to stop him. What say you sell him to me now? I pay a good price."

Rage took a hold of me. Not the red-angry kind that makes you shout – this rage filled me with an icy cold calm. I laid down my fork. Looked at him square. "I don't wish to sell. I can't manage without him."

"Didn't you hear what I said?" White Trash demanded. "You won't have no choice. The second he gets a chance, that boy will run. I've spent my life working niggers, I know their ways. You haven't broken that boy. There's a light in his eyes shouldn't be there. He's dreaming of freedom. I can smell it."

"I have faith in him," I said.

"Faith be damned! You put your trust in him and you're the biggest fool in the whole of America." Then more filth poured from his white trash lips. When at last he stopped, Whiskey Breath started up.

"You're making a mistake saying 'thank you' to your boy," he said, as serious as a preacher. "You've got to keep negroes in their place. Keep them scared. Keep them trembling. Didn't you see how I treat my boy? When I speak he darts like a streak of lightning to do my bidding."

"And if he didn't?" I asked.

Whiskey Breath smiled his slow, charming smile. "Why then, I'd skin him alive."

They went on and on. I was sick, they said. I wasn't thinking straight. I was a god-damned fool and worse if I thought I could take my boy north. After I'd finished eating I went on deck to get away from them, but Whiskey Breath took it into his head to come with me. I made the excuse that the wind was too cold on deck and went into the saloon. He followed me there too.

Seemed I'd found me a friend.

It was only when the steamboat docked in Charleston that he took his leave of me. I sure was glad to see the back of him.

When he was gone my rage was replaced by a kind of dumbstruck amazement that hit me like a blow to the head. The Captain, Whiskey Breath, White Trash – all the rest of them – had questioned my judgement. They'd questioned my sanity. But at no point had any of those men questioned that I was anything other than what I seemed to be. A gentleman.

For the first time I dared to hope that Benjamin and I were going to get away with it.

Benjamin helped me – his invalid master – down the gangway, onto shore and into a small carriage. I sat and waited while he went back for the trunk and loaded it. I was careful not to thank him.

The carriage took us to a hotel. The owner – a man by the name of Shaw – came out to meet us. When he saw the state of my health, he called for help bringing me in. I was assisted up to a room and right away I ordered my slave to the kitchen to tell the cook to rustle up some hot poultices.

By the time Benjamin got back, Mr Shaw and the folks who'd helped me up the stairs had gone. We were left to ourselves.

For a while, we just held each other close.

"We're going to get there," I whispered, over and over.

Each time I said it, he replied, "We are."

It was like being at a prayer meeting. The repeating of it put hope and courage into our hearts.

When we both felt stronger, I went down for dinner, keeping Benjamin at hand to cut up my food.

In the dining room Mr Shaw was going from table to table, talking to guests, making folks feel comfortable, keeping everyone happy. When he came to me he enquired as to where I was going and why. I told him my story about the medical man in Philadelphia, and added that I planned to take the steamer the following day.

It was then that he informed me steamers didn't run that route in the winter months.

I guess I looked real down-hearted because Mr Shaw lost no time in telling me of another way to get there. I'd need to take the Overland Mail Route, he said. I'd have to catch a steamer to Wilmington, North Carolina, and go on from there. It might take a while longer, but I'd get to Philadelphia in the end.

I thanked him for his advice and turned my attention back to my meal, but I couldn't hardly eat another mouthful. My stomach was turning over and over like a butter churn.

If we didn't get to Philadelphia before our five day pass was up we'd be in trouble.

When we didn't return to our masters, we'd be named as runaways. Notices would be put out. Telegrams would be sent. Folks would be on the look-out for us. If we weren't in Philadelphia at the end of our five days, the chances were we'd never get to freedom.

Rosa

The next morning Benjamin ordered a carriage at the hotel door, saw the trunk loaded up and then helped his sick master on board. We went on down to the Custom House on the wharf where we'd landed the day before and I asked the clerk for two tickets – one for me, one for my slave – to carry us right through to Philadelphia.

The man behind the counter was big and mean, with a face the colour of cheese. He didn't answer me, but he whistled at Benjamin like he was a dog. When Benjamin looked up Cheese Face said, "Boy, do you belong to this gentleman?"

"Yes, sir," Benjamin said.

Cheese Face grunted.

He handed the tickets over and I paid for them. But then he pushed a book towards me and said, "Here. Write your name. Your boy's, too. And I need an extra dollar duty for him."

I paid the dollar.

But I couldn't write our names – it was against the law to teach a slave to write.

With my left hand I pointed to the right that was bandaged and resting in the sling. "Would you write my name for me?" I said to Cheese Face. "As you can see, I can't manage it."

"No," he said. Flat, just like that.

That ticket office was heaving with people. The moment Cheese Face spoke, they all fell silent.

I don't know what would have happened. If I didn't sign I guess he could have refused to let us on board. The moment stretched out thin, taut. It snapped when a man pushed his way through the crowd. "What's going on?" he said.

It was Whiskey Breath, who'd taken such a liking to me on the steamer the day before. I guess he'd spent the whole night drinking in a dockside whorehouse. It was ten in the morning, but he was still staggering drunk.

He greeted me like we were old friends then asked, "Everything all right here?"

I nodded towards Cheese Face, but before I could explain, Cheese Face asked Whiskey Breath, "You know this man?"

"Know him?" Whiskey Breath threw his arm around my shoulder. I managed not to flinch. "Why, we're practically brothers!"

"You can vouch for him?"

"Yes, sir!"

It seemed that he was well known in the town and his family were highly respected. He was lying through his perfect white teeth about knowing me well, but his whiskey-soaked word carried the day.

The next thing I knew, the Captain of the steamer had stepped forward to declare, "I'll write down his name myself. I'll take full responsibility."

And so Benjamin and I were entered on the passenger list as 'Mr Butler and slave'.

We stepped aboard the steamer with the Captain apologising all the while for what had happened in the ticket office.

"It's these damned abolitionists." He spat on the deck. "There are so many Yankees trying to smuggle out valuable slaves we have to be careful. I've seen whole families detained until their identity could be verified."

I repeated a few of the cuss words I'd picked up about abolitionists on my first train ride. The Captain grinned and raised a hand as if he was going to slap me hard on the back, but then he had second thoughts about doing that to an invalid. But he was mighty pleased with me, and so I ordered Benjamin to fetch my trunk on board.

The longer I played at being a gentleman, the better I was getting. The whole of that voyage I didn't once get told I was too soft on my boy.

Rosa

We came in to Wilmington, North Carolina, the
following morning. I guess the strain was beginning
to tell on me by then because my belly was
cramping and my back was sore. It seemed I wasn't
so much playing the part of an invalid as actually
becoming one.

We boarded a train north. Some of the
compartments had couches on both sides which
were meant for families with small children, or the
elderly or the sick. The guard took one look at me
and led me to where an old man and his two adult
daughters were already sitting. After Benjamin
settled me on a couch, he was sent off to the negro
compartment.

The ladies were eager to talk, but I didn't want to encourage conversation and so I kept my replies to the minimum. When their questions dried up I stared out of the window and kept my silence.

After a while the old man stood up and took himself off down the train to stretch his legs. I was left alone with his daughters.

If I thought that travelling with men telling me how to manage my slave was bad, travelling with sympathetic women was far worse. The moment their daddy was out of the compartment, they came and sat either side of me.

I cussed myself for being so stupid. I'd spent all my life in parlours and dining rooms watching white folks talk. I'd noticed a long time ago that when a man opens his mouth and speaks his thoughts, sooner or later he shows himself up for a fool. But if a man keeps quiet, that's a whole different game. Folks start to wonder what's going through his mind. They fill his silence with their own imaginings. They figure he's a deep thinker, that he deserves respect. I'd learned when I was waiting at the dinner table that silence is a mighty weapon.

And I'd gone and used it on those ladies.

I'd meant to make myself invisible. But I'd done just the opposite.

They fluttered around me like a pair of butterflies, batting their eyelashes, asking what was wrong with me, could they make me more comfortable, could they fetch me something to ease the pain? I sighed with relief when their daddy came back, but then he started in on me too.

"Been talking to your boy," he informed me.

Oh. So that's where he went.

"He says you've got the rheumatic fever. That right?"

"That's right, sir. I'm on my way to Philadelphia. I'm told there's a doctor there can help me."

"Doctors are quacks," he said. "They'll take your money, give you nothing but sugar water for it. Here, I want you to have this. I've been writing it out for you. It's the remedy my grandmother used to ease her aching joints, bless her soul. Mighty powerful and won't cost you a dime."

He held out a piece a piece of paper towards me. Hell!

I couldn't write. And I couldn't read either.

I was thinking fast. I could pretend to, I supposed. But what if I held it the wrong way up? What if he asked me to comment on it?

The only thing I could think to do was to take it, fold it up and put it in my waistcoat pocket without looking at it.

"Why thank you, sir," I said. "That's most kind. I'll read it later if I may. Right now I'm awfully tired. I do apologise."

The ladies were all over me then, taking off their shawls, folding them up, tucking them under my head to act as a pillow, taking my coat and spreading it over me, telling me to lie back on the couch.

I shut my eyes. Forced my breathing to go slower. Deeper.

As soon as they thought I was asleep the ladies got to talking.

"Such a nice young man, Papa," one said.

"I do declare!" said the other. "Why, I've never been so taken with anyone in my life."

It was crazy! On and on they ran, talking about how charming I was, how handsome, how kind. It seemed I was the very image of the perfect Southern gentleman. I was the creature of their dreams. They started wondering aloud if they couldn't persuade me to go visit them, they were perfectly sure I could be made better if only they could care for me themselves. I figured I could have married either or both of them if I'd just crooked my little finger! And wouldn't their eyes have popped out over the breakfast table the morning after the wedding?

I hoped there would come a day when Benjamin and I would be able to laugh about it. But as I lay there on that train for what felt like an eternity, I'd never felt so mortified.

On the long list of hazards I'd imagined we might face, I'd never dreamed a pair of young ladies might fall in love with me.

A few stops down the line, their soft hands woke me up because they were getting off and they needed their shawls back. The old man pressed his calling card into my palm and told me to come visit them if I passed back that way.

"We'd be very happy to see you, sir."

I promised him that I would and he stepped off the train. The young ladies took a while to follow him. The first one bade me a tender farewell, taking my good hand and holding it in hers, pulling it so close I could almost feel her heart beating. The second did the same only she went a little further, making sure my fingers brushed against her ample bosom.

"Do come and stay," she murmured. "You'd be made so very welcome."

At last the train pulled out and left the three of them standing on the station waving at me. The ladies were dabbing the tears from their eyes, but I breathed one almighty long sigh of relief.

Yet my problems with Southern ladies were far from over.

Rosa

I'd been used to spending every minute of every day running around for Miss Abigail.

The only time I ever sat down was when I was sewing something for her – making a new dress, mending an old one. There wasn't a waking moment that I'd not had some task or other. Now there was nothing to do but stare out of the train window, fretting and praying to God to get us to Philadelphia safe. I wished I could read. There were folks around me lost in newspapers. Books. But that was yet another thing slavery had denied me. I was alone with my thoughts chasing their tails in my head.

Boredom and fear are a bad combination. I dozed a little, but the dreams I had were so troubled I was better off awake.

It got colder as we travelled north, the temperature dropping lower with each mile. I was feeling it, but at least I had my coat. All Benjamin wore were the clothes he'd had in Georgia, where it hardly ever froze, not even in the middle of winter.

I was out of my mind with worry over him when we stopped at a station. A well-dressed lady stepped into the compartment and took a seat near me. Her skirt was wide enough to fill the whole carriage. She was on the plump side, laced so tight into her dress that her bosom was thrust up to her chin. Despite the cold, sweat had made great rings under her arms. Her flesh was puffy and white, like bread dough rising in a bowl. I imagined what might happen if she got knocked. Would she collapse? Fold in on herself? I was tempted to stab her with my finger and find out.

There was a gentleman with her who had a strange accent and I wondered if he was from the north – a Yankee. He was helping her along, but he was distant and polite with her. I figured they weren't companions.

Traders selling food and drink thronged the platform and we hadn't eaten in a long while. My boy – he was such an attentive slave – was out there hunting refreshments for his master. I watched Benjamin's head bobbing through the crowds and my heart lifted at the sight of it as he started coming back to our carriage.

And that's when a scream hit me smack between the eyes.

"Runaway!"

That lump of dough in a dress had pulled down the window and was pointing right at Benjamin.

"Stop that boy! He's a runaway!"

They say time slows down when you're real scared. Or speeds up. I'd say it does both. My heart was banging so hard and fast I thought it was going to smash right out of my chest. But I seemed to have stopped breathing altogether. Pictures were flashing through my mind. One after the other. Benjamin. Whipped. Bleeding. Dying. Me. Slavers. White trash. Fingers in my flesh. Pictures flashing fast, fast, fast – so fast it made me dizzy.

But at the same time I was looking out onto the platform and things seemed to go real slow. It was like watching people in a dream. White folks had turned to see where the screams were coming from. They looked at Dough Lady. Listened to her. Slow, slow, slow, they turned their heads back towards Benjamin. Slow, slow, slow, they flowed around and surrounded him. Put hands on him. He didn't resist. But that didn't stop him getting a fist in the belly. Another full in the face.

Dough Lady was calling, "Bring him here."

And they were dragging Benjamin through the crowd. Slow, slow, slow.

She looked at the Yankee gentleman who'd helped her onto the train. His lips were pinched tight with an expression I couldn't read.

Dough Lady said, "That's my boy Samuel. Ran off a while back. Well, he's sure gonna pay for it now."

Her words came from a long way away. My fear was screaming so loud it took an age for that one word to make itself heard.

Samuel.

Samuel?

Her boy, Samuel?

Her boy?

Samuel!

That name was like ice cold water thrown in my face. She'd mistaken Benjamin for someone else!

I realised I'd been holding my breath all this time. When I opened my mouth I sucked in air like I'd just come up from the deep ocean floor.

"That's *my* boy, ma'am," I said.

Too low. She didn't hear. I cleared my throat. Loud and firm, I repeated, "That's my boy, ma'am. You're mistaken."

"What? Don't be ridiculous," she snapped. "That's Samuel. Ungrateful creature! Bring him here, bring him here."

He'd had the wind punched out of him. His head was hanging down. When I spoke his name he raised it. His lip was split. Blood was tricking down his chin.

He looked at me. His eyes were brim full of despair. But he didn't know she was mistaken. Not yet.

"Tell this lady what your name is," I said.

It came out in a croak. "Benjamin."

She squinted. Took a real close look. I thought she might go on arguing, but her fat white face collapsed.

"Oh ..." she said. "Well, I could have sworn ..."

"This boy isn't your Samuel. It's my Benjamin," I told her. "We agree on that?"

"I suppose."

I said to the folks who had hold of Benjamin, "He's no runaway. Let him go."

They were reluctant to release him. The Yankee man was telling people to leave my boy alone, but it was a long time before they backed off. And when they did, eyes were still on us. They'd spilled some of his blood. They wanted more.

I said, "What you got there, boy?"

He'd kept hold of the food he'd bought. It was crushed to pieces, but he gave it me anyway, handing it in through the window.

I knew full well that white folks blame slaves for their misfortunes.

You got whipped? You shouldn't have upset your master.

You got raped? You shouldn't have tempted him.

I snapped at Benjamin, "I'll deal with you later, boy. We're ready to move off. Get back in the nigger car. And don't you go causing any more trouble."

I threw in a few cuss words for good measure. The crowd broke up, satisfied.

We took our seats. My heart was thudding, my palms were damp. It felt like it would be a long time before I would calm myself.

The train pulled out of the station. That might have been the end of it, but Dough Lady wouldn't stop talking. She turned to me, laid a hand on my arm. Her white fingers pinching my skin. Nails pressing into the cloth of my jacket.

"Oh I hope your boy doesn't turn out to be as worthless as my Samuel," she said. "Running off like that! Why'd he do it? You know, I treated him like my own son."

Strange, the way memories catch you sometimes. Things you think are buried and long forgotten rise, clear and sharp, in your mind.

All of a sudden I was a child again, sitting on the back step one day with Miss Abigail. I must have been around three years old. I guess she was nine or ten.

The difference in our ages was enough for her to make a pet of me. When I was a baby she dressed me up like a living doll. Used to pick me up, carry me about the place.

When I started walking she taught me to act like her, speak like her. "Like a little lady," she said. I guess it was akin to having a talking parrot or a dancing dog. A monkey, dressed in human clothes. I kept her amused. But God forbid I should overstep the line.

That particular day I went too far. She was playing one of those girls' games, wondering who she was going to marry. Drawing word pictures of imaginary men with blond hair and green eyes. Tall, strong, handsome gentlemen, who'd fall in love the moment they clapped eyes on her. Who'd shower her with jewels and dresses. A man who'd die for love of her.

"I'm going to marry a Russian prince," Miss Abigail said. "Or maybe the King of England."

I wanted to join in, so I said the first thing that came into my head. "I'm going to marry the President of the United States."

The next thing I knew I was face down in the dirt. She'd hit me so hard she knocked me clean off the step and into the yard. She was sitting on my back hissing into my ear. "You'll marry a nigger. Black as coal. And you'll have a passel of nigger brats."

And now?

Why, I'd lay money on the fact that when Miss Abigail knew I'd run she'd say exactly the same as Dough Lady. I could see it as clearly as if she was standing right in front of me. A soft whisper, tears in her eyes, and a wounded look on her face. "Why'd Rosa run? We treated her so well. Like one of the family."

A wave of sickness washed over me. How could white folks tell themselves such lies? I thought of my father, pinning my mother up against the wall, lifting her skirt. Of Miss Abigail's husband, creeping between my sheets. I could smell him. Feel him. Taste him. The anger surged up in me. And the fear. I had to press my hands together to stop them shaking. I bit my lip so hard I drew blood.

Dough Lady was still chattering. She was plucking my sleeve now, looking at me with pleading eyes. She must have asked me something. God knows what. I didn't know how to reply. But it turned out I didn't need to.

The Yankee who'd helped her onto the train was staring at her, hard-faced.

In fact, he was staring at the two of us. He was mad. Real mad. At her. At me. I could see it in his eyes.

But he was holding it all in. He said, "How long ago did your Samuel run away?"

"Oh about a year," she said. "Maybe more."

The Yankee's lips had been pursed tight, like a rosebud. But now they were just a thin red line. His tone was still polite. But cold as ice. "Did Samuel have a wife?" he asked.

Dough Lady looked puzzled. "Why yes. At one time. Girl by the name of Liza. Now, she was as good and faithful a negro as anyone could wish for. But oh my! Her health wasn't none too good. It got so bad I had to get rid of her." She smiled at me, pleased with herself. "I sold her south to New Orleans. The climate there is so much better." She puffed herself up, expecting to be congratulated.

"You treated Samuel like your own son?" the Yankee said.

"Why, yes."

"I guess you'd sell your son's wife too if her health failed her?"

The mocking tone was thick as treacle but Dough Lady didn't catch on.

"This Liza ..." the Yankee went on. "She was glad of it, was she? To be sold south for the sake of her health? She thank you for that?"

"Why no!" Dough Lady exclaimed. "I never saw anyone take on the way Liza did. She made such a fuss about leaving Samuel and the little one! All her howling and sobbing nearly made my head split open."

"She had a child?" the Yankee said.

"Yes. He upped and died not long after. I should have sold him too while I had the chance. He lost me a good deal of money dying like that."

There was a silence for a while.

Then the Yankee asked, "Was Liza good looking?"

Dough Lady smiled. "Oh yes. She was real pretty. And fair skinned too, you know, with good straight hair. Pale as me, almost. She'll have no trouble getting another husband."

I winced. I knew that if Liza was pretty and pale skinned a slave owner would buy her for his own pleasure, his own use. If her new master had a wife she'd choose not to see it, just like Miss Abigail. The thought made me sick to the stomach, but what was surprising was that the Yankee didn't look any happier than I felt.

"I made sure to tell the trader to find her a good master," Dough Lady said. "She had no right to upset me so with all her wailing." She started to sniffle, reaching into her bag for a lace handkerchief that she dabbed her eyes with. I watched her try to squeeze some tears out, but that handkerchief stayed dry.

There was another silence.

The Yankee wasn't saying anything, but I could see his temper building. He was like an engine with a head of steam. Any second now he'd blow.

I'd never seen a white man get mad on a slave's behalf. I was stumped. I couldn't figure him out at all. But then it dawned on me that maybe, just maybe, he was an abolitionist. Could he be? I'd never seen one before. The way folks in the South talked you'd have thought they all had horns and a tail and breathed fire down their noses.

The Yankee leaned forward, and Dough Lady fluttered her eyelashes, thinking he was going to comfort her.

But he said, "Liza was a good girl, you say. Faithful. Loyal. Don't you think it might have been kinder to set her free?"

Dough Lady recoiled, jerking back in her seat as if flames and clouds of smoke were billowing from his nostrils. "What on earth for?" She opened her fan and started flapping it. "I have no patience with people who turn their slaves free." She was huffing and puffing now. "Why, my own husband wanted all his freed when he died. But he wasn't in his right mind. I tore up his will after he took his last breath. He couldn't possibly have meant to do something so unfair."

It came hurtling out of my mouth before I could stop it. "Unfair to you or to them?"

She was taken aback at my tone. So was the Yankee. He looked at me, an eyebrow raised, surprised but kind of pleased. It was like he thought I might have sympathy for the abolitionist cause. Heck! I couldn't have anyone on the train thinking that!

Dough Lady was twittering. "Unfair to them, of course! Everyone knows slaves can't take care of themselves! They need looking after. Like children. They're our responsibility. Turning them loose? Why, it's crazy!" She sniffed, then added, "Not that they know what's good for them. I've had ten or more run off since my husband died."

The Yankee coughed. At least, I think he did. It sounded to me like a cuss word came out right along with the phlegm. "You're wrong, ma'am," he said. "My own grandmother freed her slaves before she died. They're in Ohio now and doing very well. I've seen them myself."

"That can't be true," she snapped. "Freed slaves are as miserable as sin. That's a well-known fact."

"If that's the case no doubt yours will come back to you," he said. "Samuel will return some day soon and beg for your forgiveness."

"I shall whip him for running off. If I ever get my hands on him, why I'll flay the hide off his bones ...!"

The Yankee said quietly, "Your husband must be turning in his grave, ma'am." He looked at me. "Wouldn't you agree, sir?"

I wanted to say yes. Wanted to talk to him some more. But how could I? I had to make him think I was no better than she was.

"You misunderstand me," I said, and my voice was cold. "I'm with the lady, sir. It is sheer folly to free niggers."

No one in that carriage spoke again. And the Yankee got off at the next stop without a backward glance.

December
24th, 1848
Night

Rosa

Train, steamer. Steamer, train. Train, steamer. On and on. We'd left Macon, Georgia, on Wednesday. We arrived at Baltimore, Maryland late on Saturday. It was December 24th. Christmas Eve.

Baltimore was the last big slave port between us and freedom. From there we could catch the train to Philadelphia. By morning we'd belong to no one but ourselves.

We were so close. But the closer we got, the tighter my nerves were strung. Any second now, I was going to snap.

There had been no time for Benjamin and me to be alone together that day. No moments for us to be soothed or to gather strength from each other. No chance to whisper, "You all right?" No time to lie, "I'm fine." Travelling had made me bone tired. Pretending to be a white man had brought me to the brink of breaking. And now, with the scent of freedom in the air, the hope that we'd make it – and the fear we wouldn't – turned me feverish. By the time we reached Baltimore I was real sick.

Folks were watchful there. Even more than they'd been the rest of the way. I could feel eyes searing into my skin, peeling away the layers of clothing, seeing who and what I was underneath. I was careful not to smile. Not to be kind. To treat Benjamin with the contempt folks expected white to show black.

When we found the train to Philadelphia, Benjamin helped me into a compartment and then went to the negro carriage. I settled back in my seat. The platform was a riot of noise and hustle. Any minute now the train would depart. By five the following morning, we'd be there. We'd be free. There was just this one last night to endure. This one last night I had to pretend.

Pictures started running through my mind. Pictures of me and Benjamin. Of the children we'd have. Our children. He would never have to think twice about whether he was their daddy. We would never have to fear they'd be sold.

I was so lost in those pictures that when Benjamin's face appeared before me I smiled.

He didn't smile back. For a moment I wondered why.

Then I saw he wasn't alone. There was a man at his back. A man in the shadows.

A man who I prayed to God hadn't seen me smile.

I realised that we were still on that platform. Still in Baltimore. Still on the run.

"I been stopped," Benjamin said. "The conductor here says there's a problem. We got to go to the ticket office."

And so I got off the train and went to the counter. "You wanted to see me?" I said to the man there.

My heart was in my throat. I thought this was it. Our owners had met. Bumped into each other in the street, maybe. Found out that neither of us were where we'd said we'd be. They knew we'd run. And this man was about to give the order for our arrest. He had the eyes of a hawk. Or an eagle. There was something of the hunter in that face – something cold and clever, something deadly.

"Yes, I did," he said, real slow. There was a long pause while he looked me up and down. I was expecting him to say my name. To call me Rosa. Runaway slave, property of Mr Cornwell of Macon, Georgia.

But all he said was, "It's against our rules, taking a slave along to Philadelphia, unless you can prove you've got a right to do it."

He didn't know who we were! I was relieved, but only for a moment. "Why's that?" I asked.

"If we allow a gentleman to take a slave past here and that man turns out not to be his rightful owner, why then we're liable," Eagle Eye explained. "If the real owner comes along and proves his boy escaped along our railroad, we have to pay compensation. We can't let your boy ride that train unless you can prove he belongs to you."

There were people all around us watching, listening. I caught one or two whispers –

"He looks real sick."

"Reckon he's going to faint at any moment."

My mouth opened but nothing came out. My mind was a big, blank sheet.

"Do you know anyone in Baltimore who can vouch for you?" Eagle Eye said.

"No I don't," I replied, trying to gather my wits. "I bought tickets in Charleston to carry the two of us right through to Philadelphia. I'm on my way to see a doctor. You can't keep us here."

"I can and I will."

I looked at Benjamin. Benjamin looked at me, then dropped his eyes to the floor. We both knew that our five day passes would expire tomorrow.

When we didn't return, the word would be out. If they detained us here in Baltimore, if they made enquiries, we were sure to be discovered.

Neither of us knew what to say or do. We were out of ideas.

But there's something about a train that's due to leave – an excitement in the air, an impatience that's kind of catching. There were other passengers in that office and they were looking angry. Irritated. But not with me.

"You're very pale, sir," one of them said. "Are you feeling quite well?"

I realised then that the crowd's sympathy was with me. I was a sick man, a respectable gentleman, being stopped from making a journey. To a doctor. On Christmas Eve. When peace and goodwill are supposed to reign.

"No, I'm not well," I said. "I'm not well at all."

I let the sickness I'd been holding at bay wash over me. My knees buckled. If Benjamin hadn't caught me, I'd have been flat out on the floor.

The onlookers cried out. There were murmurs, then hostile stares at the man who was stopping me travelling.

"He's sick, sir."

"Can't you see this gentleman needs to get on that train?"

Eagle Eye started to bend and buckle in the heat of their glares. His hand went to his head. "I don't know," he said. "Company rules ..."

"Rules be damned, sir," someone said. "You can see for yourself this man's not well. Let him go, for pity's sake."

There was a pause.

The scream of the train whistle.

The groan of pain that escaped me then was real. Fear had clutched my belly and was squeezing it so tight I thought I'd never stand straight again.

And then Eagle Eye was sending his clerk running. "Tell the conductor to wait." He turned. "Go get on board. Fast as you can, now."

We pushed our way through the crowds, Benjamin half carrying, half dragging me. He threw me into a compartment and sprinted for the negro carriage just as the train moved off. I stood and craned my neck out the window, wanting to see him get on, but the crowds and the steam from the engine were too thick.

Sweat was pouring down my face, my neck, my back, but I felt cold as ice. I huddled down in my corner. It was a long, long time before my teeth stopped chattering.

Rosa

We finally left Baltimore at about eight in the evening. As far as I knew it was a straight run from there to Philadelphia. We were due to arrive at five the following morning. All down the train the other passengers settled themselves for the night, but I couldn't. I'd hardly slept at all since we'd started running, but even though I was bone weary there was too much feeling flowing through my veins for me to rest.

When we reached a place called Havre de Grace, Maryland, we hissed to a stop. And it was then that a guard came along the platform telling us all to get out.

It seemed there was a wide river to cross. We all had to leave the train, get on a ferryboat and then board a second train on the other side.

I stepped out of the compartment. It was dark and there was a chill wind blowing off the water. Rain was falling. Freezing cold daggers of it.

And, for the first time, there was no Benjamin waiting to help me. I looked to the left. To the right. There was no sign of him – none at all.

I'd held myself together so well. But now I felt a fear rising in my throat that I couldn't contain. Where in the hell was he? What in the name of God had happened to him? All kinds of things flashed through my head. Slave catchers had got him. Or traders. He'd been thrown off the train. Stabbed. Killed. Murdered.

As the conductor went past I said, "Seen my boy?"

A smile curled his lip. A teasing, tormenting kind of sneer. "Why no," he said, real slow. "I haven't seen him since Baltimore."

I figured he was the second abolitionist I'd ever met. "What?" I said.

"I ain't even sure he got on the train," the conductor told me. "I figure maybe he's run off, don't you?"

"He wouldn't do that."

"Oh, you'd be surprised how strong freedom tugs when folk get within sniffing distance of it," the conductor drawled. "He's probably run all the way to Philadelphia by now."

"No ... no ..." I was clutching at his coat. "Find him for me. Find him."

He prised my fingers off his jacket.

"I'm no slave-hunter, sir," he said, sharp now. "Find your own god-damned boy."

I couldn't move. Terror nailed me to the spot. Panic had its hand around my throat and was squeezing the life out of me. I knew damned well that there were white men who'd kill a black one for sport. Something real bad had happened if Benjamin wasn't here.

He had to be dead. And if he was dead, what was the point of me being alive?

I wanted to scream. I wanted to yell. To beg the Lord to take me right there, right then.

But I had a child in my belly. A child that might be Benjamin's.

I tried to breathe slow. To make myself think. Passengers were going ahead of me. Getting on that ferry. I needed to go with them.

I couldn't without my husband! What should I do? Stay here until I found him? Where? Find a hotel? How in the heck could I pay for it? Benjamin had all our money. We thought we'd been so smart.

Seemed to us that the very last place thieves would look would be a slave's pockets. I didn't have a cent on me. And if I stayed out in the open I'd freeze to death before dawn.

All I could do was board that ferry. Get on the train on the other side. Hope and pray that Benjamin was alive. That he'd find me.

And if he didn't?

That night was one of the worst I'd ever known. I felt so afraid. So alone. A life without Benjamin in it was no life at all. I prayed myself ragged. Did deals with God. Bring him back, and I'll ... what? I had nothing to bargain with.

We crossed the river and got on the other train. I kept watching. Kept waiting. There was nothing else I could do. We didn't move for a long time. I couldn't see anything of what was going on but I could hear a lot of clunking and crashing and then, at last, we were moving again.

I don't know how long I sat, staring out at the freezing darkness. Time passes slower when you're that scared.

It may only have been a few minutes. But it didn't feel like it. It felt like years.

Centuries.

And then I heard his voice.

Soft.

Gentle.

Warm.

"I'm here."

Back in Macon, I once saw a child run out in front of a galloping horse. The animal reared up, throwing the rider into the dirt, breaking his arm. The child wasn't harmed, but the shock he gave his mother was fearful bad. When they brought him back to her I'd expected her to hug him tight. Squeeze him so hard she'd crack his ribs. But she didn't.

She was so mad at him for scaring her half to death she boxed his ears. His head must have been ringing for days. I didn't understand her reaction then but I understood it on that train. Because when Benjamin appeared before me – not bruised, not bloodied, not broken – I was so angry I slapped him full across the face.

"Where in the name of God have you been?"

"Sorry, master. Sorry."

My right hand was bandaged and in a sling. I'd smacked him with the left so it wasn't a hard blow, but soon as I'd done it I felt weak with shame.

Seemed he'd fallen asleep. That was all. He'd curled up in among the trunks and cases and he'd sparked right out. The luggage vans had been rolled onto the boat and rolled off on the other side, he

73

said. He'd slept through the entire thing. Benjamin only found out we'd crossed a river when the conductor shook him awake and told him his master was out of his mind with fury, thinking he'd run off.

Benjamin went back to the luggage van, cowering and cringing like a good slave. I sat, staring into the dark.

I dozed a little. I dreamed I was back there. The master, sliding his hand under the sheet, pulling it off of me. Only this time I didn't kneel down and I didn't keep quiet like he told me to.

This time I screamed and hollered. This time I cussed him for what he was. Cussed Miss Abigail for refusing to see what her husband was doing. Cussed her mother for giving me away in the first place. Cussed my father, for allowing her to rip me from my mother. For breaking both our hearts.

My screaming was so loud it woke me up. But then I realised I hadn't made a sound. It wasn't me. It was the train. Whistling. Over and over.

It was still dark outside. But there were lights in the distance. And down along the length of the train, folks were stirring. I heard one man call to another, "Wake up. We're coming into Philadelphia."

If I thought it had been hard to control my feelings before, it was nothing to how it was when the train pulled up in the station. Almost before the

brakes had stopped their squealing, Benjamin had
come to help me. He was fighting so hard to keep
the smile from his face, to keep the joy from shining
out of his eyes. I could feel him itching to catch
me in his arms and hold me close. But there were
still plenty of Southerners around – folks who would
have dragged us back without a moment's thought.
Our act, our pretence couldn't change. Not yet. But
oh Lord! How hard it was to behave like an invalid
traveller and his loyal slave when both our hearts
were yelling –

"Free!"

"Free!"

"FREE!"

PART 3

Rosa

I'd been right about that train conductor. He was
an abolitionist. After he'd woken Benjamin in the
luggage van, he'd told him where to go and who
to see if he wanted to escape from his master. As
soon as we were out of the station we climbed into
a carriage and went straight to the Philadelphia
boarding house the conductor had named.

My heart was thumping "free!" with each beat,
but the rest of my body was doing something
entirely different. I was shaking like a leaf the
whole of that ride. When the carriage pulled up and
we climbed the steps to the boarding house, my legs
started to fail me. The moment we were inside, the
moment the door shut behind us, I was overcome
with dizziness. Benjamin and Mr Weston – the

owner of the boarding house – had to carry me upstairs and lay me on the bed. Then Mr Weston told Benjamin to follow him to the kitchen and fetch me some broth. While they were down there, he whispered, "You looking for your freedom, son?"

"Yes."

"Is that your master upstairs?"

"No."

Benjamin had been too concerned about me to explain more. He came back up with the broth and spooned it into my mouth like I was a child. It was good, nourishing food, but it was an hour or more before I felt strong enough to stand. When I did, I took off my gentleman's clothes and put on my dress.

I hated doing that.

It stank of Miss Abigail. It stank of her house. Of him.

And I vowed that the very first thing I'd do – now we were free – was sew myself a brand new dress.

As soon as I was changed, we went downstairs.

When Mr Weston saw me I guess he figured I was a white man wearing a woman's clothes because his eyes almost popped clean out of his head. He had to sit himself down.

"I am a woman, sir," I reassured him. "I had to dress as a gentleman to get us out."

His mouth opened and closed like a fish. At last he said, "That was mighty bold. Why, I don't believe I've ever heard of anything so brave. And you did all that to bring one slave to freedom? I salute you, ma'am."

"Not one slave," I said. "Two."

He was puzzled by that. "Where's the other? Don't tell me you had a child hidden in that trunk?"

"No, sir," I said. "I am the other slave. Benjamin is my husband."

It was a strange thing to see the way that man's face changed when he realised I had black blood running in my veins.

Mr Weston was an abolitionist – there was no doubting that. He was a good, kind man but there was a shift in his attitude when he grasped that I wasn't white. He still spoke to me polite. He was still astounded by my bravery. He was still kind. And he helped us. But it was in the way that a man might take in a stray dog or an injured bird. Not in the way you'd treat a fellow human being. An equal.

It was so subtle, that tilt, I wondered if I'd imagined it. I thought maybe these last few days had clouded my mind. But later – when Mr Weston sent messages out to his abolitionist friends and we found ourselves surrounded by curious white folks – I saw that same look on their faces too. A tiny shift in the way they looked at me that made me wince like I'd been stung.

They were pleasant enough people, I guess, yet I couldn't feel comfortable around any of them. I suppose I didn't believe in the goodness of white folks, any more than I believed in goblins or fairies. I expected them to turn on us, to say they'd been fooling, that now it was time to take us back to our owners. But as they sat there in Mr Weston's parlour they were full of helpful advice and information. We'd been planning on travelling to Canada and settling there, but when Benjamin said that there was a chorus of –

"No!"

"Don't go there!"

"That would be a bad idea."

Canada was a cold, cold, cold country they said. People who'd grown up in the heat of Georgia like we had would find the climate impossible to bear. At last, Benjamin and I agreed that Boston would be our final destination.

But we didn't go there right away.

That night, in that Philadelphia boarding house, I lost the baby I was carrying.

All those cramps that I'd put down to fear? All that weakness and dizziness? It was the baby coming loose inside of me, like a little boat coming adrift from its moorings.

Maybe it was a blessing. Whatever Benjamin said, it would have been hard for him to look at a child hoping it was his, but fearing that it wasn't. And if it had come out looking like my master ... Could I have loved it? Perhaps it was better not to know.

1849
Boston

Rosa

Being free was like nothing I'd ever imagined. It was like being born again. Like growing into someone new. We were children, learning to walk in a wondrous landscape that neither of us knew or understood.

Of course that meant that sometimes we fell flat on our faces. There were plenty of things to catch us out, to trip us up. There were times folks took me for a white woman who was living with a black man. In a country where marriage between the races was illegal it caused us all kinds of trouble. If I'd ever thought the north was the Promised Land, flowing with milk and honey, I soon discovered otherwise.

There were shop-keepers who wouldn't serve us, there were strangers who'd jostle us in the street, people who'd spit in both our faces.

But these were small problems, mostly. Flies in the jam. Pick those out, and there was such a deep joy to being free it's hard to put it into words. There were the big things, of course. The obvious things. No masters. No whips. No getting bought or sold. But besides that there was a mass of tiny things. Ordinary things, I expect, if you were white. Things that delighted me every moment of every day.

Like going to bed each night with my husband at my side. Feeling the warmth of him in the dark, hearing his breath. Knowing that his face would be the first one I saw in the morning, that his voice would be the first thing I'd hear. Knowing that I'd see him every single day. That I didn't have to ask permission.

There was cooking the food we chose to eat. Wearing clothes we chose to wear. Working for people we chose to work for. Making choices for ourselves, living our lives the way we wanted.

Benjamin was a fine carpenter and I was good with a needle and thread. He got himself a job as a cabinet maker. I took in sewing. We worked almost as hard as ever but we were paid for our labour and treated well by folks who spoke to us polite. And the money we earned we could keep for ourselves. We made plenty enough to get by.

On top of all that we were learning to read and write too. My oh my, it was a struggle, but it was worth it. To be able to open a book, to be able to understand the words on the page felt like nothing short of a miracle.

The abolitionists who'd advised us to go to Boston had given us the names and addresses of people who helped us when we arrived. White folks. Black folks. Freemen. Escaped slaves. They were all eager to hear our story of how we'd got to freedom. We were invited to take coffee with them. Dine with them.

Word got around and one afternoon a churchman by the name of Reverend Wilkins came to our lodgings and asked if we'd speak at a public meeting.

The idea was terrifying. We'd escaped. But to stay safe, I figured we needed to keep quiet. Be out of sight. Invisible.

I shook my head at Benjamin, but he said, "We've got a story to tell, Rosa. An important one."

Then the Reverend started talking to Benjamin about the iniquities of slavery and the importance of publicity and how white folks needed to hear from people like us if the abolitionists were ever going to achieve their goal.

All the time the men were talking I was thinking – it'll never happen. You really think masters are going to give up their slaves just because a few Yankees tell them to?

But – without asking me – Benjamin said we'd do it.

After the Reverend had gone and I protested, he said, "We can play a part in this, Rosa. This isn't about us. It's about all those others. The ones who can't speak out, the ones who can't escape. It may be a small thing, but it's something we can do for them."

My husband looked at me, and I knew what he was saying. He was reminding me of my mother. And of the unknown girl my master would have bought to take my place. Of all the slaves, men, women and children, living much worse lives even than that.

I nodded. I agreed. Seemed I didn't have a whole lot of choice.

When the evening of that public meeting came I was a mess of nerves. It was a bone-cold chilling night. The kind that makes you feel like you're breathing in splinters of ice. Inside, the hall was hot and stuffy, but I couldn't stop my teeth from clacking together.

We followed the Reverend down the hall to the front. I took my place on the stage beside Benjamin. Folks were craning their necks for a look at us. White women were whispering behind their fans. I couldn't hear them, but I could imagine well enough what they were muttering. I'd overheard enough comments on enough street corners to know they'd be exclaiming about the straightness of my hair, the paleness of my skin, the darkness of Benjamin's. The fact that we were man and wife. Lord alone knows what kind of pictures they were making in their heads. The idea of us being together excited and repelled them in just about equal measure.

We'd decided that Benjamin and I would take it in turns to speak. We'd tell a part each.

But when I looked out at that sea of faces – some of them black but most of them white, some of them women, but most of them men – my voice dried up. It was nothing like being on an auction stand waiting to be sold. It truly wasn't. And yet ...

Hell!

My head might tell me that the folks out there were good people. My heart and my stomach disagreed. I wanted to run. I had to dig my nails into my hand to stop myself.

I had to whisper in Benjamin's ear, "You do the talking for both of us."

And he did.

When he spoke there was a fire in his belly. His words flowed sweet and smooth like honey. He held those white folks in the palm of his brown hand. They sighed with sympathy when he told them about the lives we'd lived before we'd run. They laughed at the tale of the Southern ladies who fell in love with me. They gasped in horror when Dough Lady called him 'runaway'. They cheered when he told them about us reaching Philadelphia. And when he finished with our arrival in Boston, they stood and hollered and chanted "Freedom!"

That audience was delighted with him. And so, after that, more invitations came in. My husband made something of a name for himself as a public speaker. There were meetings. Protests. Rallies. Demonstrations.

Over and over again Benjamin told white folks how we'd escaped by hiding right under their noses. They applauded us for our courage and our cleverness.

I went along to all the meetings. I was happy to sit on stage beside my husband and listen to him tell our story over and over, but I never did speak at any of them.

1850
Boston

Rosa

Benjamin and I had been living in Boston for almost two years. We were settled. Happy. Surrounded by friends. I was with child again and there was no doubting that this one was Benjamin's. We were looking forward to being a family. My husband had carved a beautiful cradle. I was sewing baby clothes.

And then Congress passed the Fugitive Slave Act.

With one stroke of a pen our liberty was taken from us. A few lines of ink on a page and everything we'd built up was smashed into pieces.

Benjamin came home one afternoon looking as sick as a dog. It had been a long time since I'd seen that look on his face.

"What's the matter?" I asked.

He slapped a pamphlet down on the table but he didn't give me time to read it.

He was so spitting mad he had to talk.

"They've passed a new law," he said. "Means our owners can come and get us any time they damn well please."

"But we're in a free state!" I replied.

"It doesn't matter. You know what else the Act says? Anyone who helps a runaway – anyone at all – will be going against the law. They could get themselves arrested too."

It was like getting a fist in the belly. I felt as sick as he looked.

We should have lain low, I thought. Shouldn't have trusted any of them. Should have kept our heads down. Stayed quiet. Been invisible. Our masters wouldn't have known where we were then. They wouldn't have been able to find us. But now? There wasn't a soul in Boston who didn't know who we were and who we'd run from.

"We've got to leave," I said. "Now."

Benjamin couldn't keep still. He was pacing up and down. "This is our home," he said. "We're not running again. The law's crazy. We can fight it."

"Not on our own," I said.

"We've got friends," he said. "Abolitionists. They'll risk themselves for us …"

I was shaking my head. I could see how it was. Why couldn't he?

"Sure," I said. "They'll risk themselves. And they might get themselves fined as a result. They might even go to prison, for a time. But they won't get whipped. They won't get raped. They won't get sold. They won't get killed. The only folks who are going to suffer are folks like us. Same way we always have."

"Rosa, we've got friends," Benjamin said. "They won't let us be taken."

"They won't have any choice."

"They'll stand up for us. They'll fight this with us."

"Benjamin, listen to me." I stood in front of him. Took his face in my hands. "They're good people. I know that. But friends or not, they're *white*. They can write letters, hold meetings, make speeches. But it's not their hides on the line. It doesn't matter what any of them say or do. We're on our own. We've got to get out of here."

I didn't want to see my husband collapse in on himself like that, but he did.

He knew I was speaking sense.

"What are we going to do?" he said.

"We've got to run again."

"Where to?" he asked. "Canada?"

"That's not far enough," I said. My mind was racing. "Seems nowhere on this continent is safe. We need to get off it. Go to England, maybe."

Benjamin walked out on me then. He left the house and it was the first time he'd ever gone away without a sweet smile and a kiss. The slamming of the door echoed in my head. We'd never fought before. Never had an angry or a bitter word.

The hours stretched out long and weary. I hadn't ever felt so sad. So beaten. The whole damned world seemed set against us. All we wanted to do was live. Where? Where could we do that?

Benjamin was back at first light. "There's a boat sails to England in a couple of weeks," he said. His voice was cracked with sadness. He took me in his arms and we rocked each other. Rocked and soothed. "We'll get ourselves a passage on that."

We should have run right away.

The ink on the Fugitive Slave Act wasn't even dry when our old masters sent agents to Boston with warrants for our arrest.

The first I knew of it was when the wife of one of our abolitionist friends came hammering on the door.

"You've got to get out," she cried. "They're coming for you."

Fear squeezed my belly, clutching my baby in its cold fist.

"Benjamin ..." I said. He was out working and I didn't know where. But I couldn't go without him!

"We've got people looking for Benjamin," she told me. "Come with me now. Now! There's no time to argue, Rosa."

So I left with her. She took me to her home and hid me there.

But they couldn't find Benjamin. When he finished his day's work, he came back to an empty house.

He was calling my name, looking for me, wondering where in the heck I'd got to when the catchers came banging on the door.

He had the sense not to open it. And they had the sense not to try breaking it down. Their noise and shouting attracted attention. Before long a crowd of abolitionists was gathered outside, swearing they'd not let Benjamin be taken. My husband sat all that night with a loaded pistol pointed at the door. Whether he'd have used it on the catchers or on himself is hard to say.

But they could bide their time. The law was on their side. Towards dawn it started to rain and the catchers took themselves to their beds.

When he was sure they'd gone, Benjamin unbolted the door and ran from the house. We were re-united at sunrise after the longest night of both our lives.

But what to do next? We couldn't get on a ship. Not in Boston harbour. The moment we set foot on deck the warrants against us would have been served. The catchers would take us back.

And we'd both sworn to die rather than let that happen.

It seemed the only way to get to England was by making the long, hard journey overland to Halifax, Canada. If we could get across the border, we could sail from there.

It was the fall and the weather was biting cold. Neither of us were in good health when we left Boston. And, every step of that journey, bad luck snapped at our heels.

We left in secret, in the dead of night, with only the clothes on our backs and all the money we possessed stuffed into a pouch. We took the first train that headed north.

We made it as far as Portland. But when we got there we found the steamer we'd planned to take had run headlong into another ship the day before. A big hole had been torn in its side and it needed mending. Three days we had to wait for it to be repaired. Three days we sat there, flinching at every sudden noise, every unexpected movement.

We were twitchy as a pair of mice who can smell a cat on the prowl.

When at last we got on board that boat it carried us safe to New Brunswick. We had reached Canada without being arrested and that was something of a relief. I guess we should have felt safe, but we didn't. In our time in Boston we'd heard plenty of tales of freeborn men and women being snatched by slavers and dragged south to be sold. It was only a line on a map that separated the United States from Canada. It would be easy enough for our owners to pay men willing to take us back by force, border or no border.

Until we'd got the ocean between us and them I wouldn't sleep easy.

We'd docked so late we missed the steamer to Windsor, Nova Scotia. We had to wait another two long days.

From Windsor we took a coach towards Halifax. And it was then that we discovered that even though slavery had been abolished in the British Empire, not everyone was overjoyed about it. Some had the same kind of foolish thoughts that clouded minds and twisted hearts in the American South.

The driver of the coach wouldn't let "no damned nigger" ride inside with his other passengers.

Neither of us had the strength for a fight, so Benjamin had to sit on top in the freezing rain. We were still seven miles short of the town when the wheels hit a deep rut and the whole coach was turned on its side.

We were all thrown every which way. Benjamin landed right on top of the driver who'd made him ride on the roof, which gave us both some satisfaction. But it was short lived. They couldn't right the coach. We had to walk through the mud and the rain those seven long miles into the town. And when at last we got there, we found the ship we'd hoped to board had sailed for England two hours before.

Rosa

There would be other ships, of course – in days, or maybe weeks. But meantime we had to stay somewhere. We were bone weary, frozen and soaked to the skin. The only place that was open when we trudged into town was a run-down hog pit of an inn. I went ahead because I knew that if Benjamin asked for a room they'd likely find themselves full up.

I asked for a bed for myself and my husband. After I paid for it Benjamin came in and all six of the landlady's chins hit the floor.

We ordered food, and she said we had to take it in our room. We were happy to shut ourselves away. But as we ate we could hear folks downstairs roaring and cussing about being under the same roof as a "filthy nigger and his white whore". It wasn't any kind of surprise when the landlady came the next day and told us we had to leave.

"I have no prejudice myself," she said, and she turned as purple as a beetroot. "I've always been a friend to the negroes. It's not me, really it isn't. It's my customers. But I can't afford to lose them. You know how it is."

Oh yes. We knew how it was.

Benjamin stood up. Smiled. She turned a deeper shade of purple.

"Ma'am," Benjamin said, with mocking sincerity. "I'm mighty glad to hear you're a friend to folks like us. That warms my heart, believe me. And I'd sure hate to go scaring your customers away." He looked across at me. "I had no idea people in these parts were so timid, did you?"

"No, I didn't," I said. "Poor creatures. What a terrible thing it must be for them to live in such fear."

Benjamin carried on. "We'd be happy to move out, ma'am."

The landlady breathed a sigh of relief, but Benjamin wasn't done yet.

He sat back down. "Yes, ma'am. If you can just find us a nice comfortable place to go to we'll be out of here right away."

The landlady didn't get back until well after noon. She'd walked the length and breadth of the town and every guest house, every inn, every hotel, every place that took in boarders was full to the rafters. So they said.

"Astounding," Benjamin declared. "This place is more crowded than Bethlehem on that first Christmas Eve. I wonder where all those folk are hiding? The town looks half empty to my eyes."

With a trembling hand our beetroot-faced landlady handed Benjamin a list.

"It's the names of all the coloured folks hereabouts," she said. "Maybe one of them might take you in?"

One did. The Reverend Jackson housed us and fed us for two weeks while we were stuck in Halifax waiting for a ship to carry us to England. We'd both been unwell when we left Boston. And the people who'd said we'd find the climate in Canada hard to bear were right. That journey to Halifax had given us colds that turned into fevers.

We couldn't afford a doctor.

By the time we got on board the ship I was so sick that Benjamin feared I wouldn't last the crossing.

I did.

But I lost the baby on the way.

Another child of mine came adrift on a rising tide of fear.

And that time it wasn't a blessing in disguise.

I grieved for that child. I grieved bitterly. Not just for the baby I wouldn't hold in my arms. I grieved for the person it might have grown up to be. For the life it might have lived. The children it might have had. For the grandchildren that would never be born. That lost baby left a hole and, in the dark of the night when I'd wake and the rest of the world was sleeping, it felt so wide and so deep I thought I'd never feel whole again.

Rosa

England was good to us.

Sure, there were some shop-keepers that wouldn't serve us. Some hotels that refused us rooms.

But the rest of the white folks we met thought Benjamin and I were exotic creatures all the way from the United States of America, with a thrilling story to tell. When word got around about how we'd escaped, we were fussed over, flattered. We'd settled in London, but Benjamin was asked to speak in town halls and theatres up and down the country. Other than that, we lived much the same the way we had in Boston. We did well for ourselves and we were happy.

Mostly.

In the day, when it was light, I was fine. But in the dark, I was haunted by the past. I'd wake in a cold sweat, thinking I was back in Georgia.

And then one night I dreamed of the time we'd first arrived in England. Our ship had docked in Liverpool. I was real sick and grieving so bad for our lost child. We were out of money, and the only lodging we could find was in a boarding house where the wind knived between the cracks in the windows and the rain dripped through the roof into puddles on the floor.

I dreamed I was lying on the bed in that hell-hole of a place.

And Miss Abigail was in the room with me, looking around.

"You ran all that way for this?" Her head was on one side, her face gentle, kind, but a little puzzled. "Why'd you do it? You had your own room at home. It was neat. Clean." She started to whine. "I don't understand how you could treat me so bad, Rosa. I miss you. I can't find a girl who sews as nice. Why'd you leave me like that? Didn't I always treat you kind?"

I wanted to speak. To tell her what I'd never been able to. To describe the nights her husband had forced me to do the things she wouldn't. To remind her of the times she'd slapped me because she was in a temper. But I couldn't find the words.

"I gave you such pretty things," she sighed. "You had all my dresses when I was done with them. Don't you recall?"

I still couldn't speak.

And then in came her mother. She just appeared, the way folk do in dreams. And she was mixed up with the Dough Lady on the train whose boy Samuel ran away, even though she'd treated him like her own son.

"No good will come of it," Dough Lady said. "Niggers don't know what's good for them. Rosa will starve to death, you'll see. She'll be begging you to take her back. Don't do it is my advice. She's got to learn the hard way."

I couldn't find my voice. All those years when I'd had to keep my head down and my mouth shut, when nothing more than a "Yes'm" could safely leave my lips, had sealed them tight. They might as well have been stitched together.

And then into the dream came a sound from the outside. A sound from the real world leaking in. I heard a child.

My child.

Our baby boy.

Born on England's soil. Not crying. Calling. Calling because he'd woken up and he could see the moon and stars out of the window. Calling because he wanted to share the wonder of it.

But I couldn't wake up. I couldn't leave the dream. Not yet.

Because hearing my child's voice made me find my own.

I stared at those two white women. I drew myself up. Stood tall.

"Look at me," I said. "Look at me good. I'm not starving. I'm not struggling. I've got my home. I've got my loving husband – the best man who ever drew breath on this earth. I've got my child. And no man is ever going to own his hide. I'm a rich woman. Richer than either of you will ever be, because I came from nothing. I thank the Lord every minute of every day for every last little thing, for every sweet breath I draw, every ray of sun that warms my skin, every puff of wind that cools it. And even if we had nothing – if we were lying naked in the gutter – do you know what? You could offer to feed me until my belly burst, you could say you'd dress me in silk and velvet – hell, you could even promise to pay me! I wouldn't take any of it. I'm free. And I'd rather starve to death with my family in England than ever come back and be a slave in America."

Their mouths popped open – two round circles of astonishment. They didn't speak. They couldn't. While I watched, they thinned and faded to nothing. Invisible.

I made them invisible.

With my words I destroyed them both.

When I woke, I knew that was that. They wouldn't be haunting my dreams again. Not ever.

I went to my child, picked him out of his cradle and carried him to the window.

Our chattering woke up Benjamin. He came and joined us.

Bathed in moonlight, we all looked up at the stars.

About **Passing for White**

Passing for White is a work of fiction inspired by the real-life escape of William and Ellen Craft from slavery in America's Deep South. I've always found their story inspiring because there were no 'white saviours' involved – they, and they alone, can take the credit.

Their plan required great ingenuity and extraordinary courage, particularly on Ellen's part. For an illiterate female slave to travel a thousand miles successfully impersonating a white gentleman was a truly remarkable achievement.

The details of their escape are described in their book *Running a Thousand Miles for Freedom*. Both their names are on the cover, but it is William who tells their story and we don't get to hear Ellen's voice directly at all. In *Passing for White*, I focus on her side – and in doing so I've drawn heavily on their journey, the people she met and the conversations she had.

Benjamin and Rosa's escape is based on real-life events, but the couple's first meeting, their relationship, the abuse by Rosa's master and her two lost babies are all entirely fictional.

The language

Offensive terms such as 'nigger', 'boy' and 'negro' were all in common use when William and Ellen Craft escaped from slavery. To not use them at all seemed to me to be a dishonest 'cleaning up' and softening of a brutal and sickening reality. I have, however, used the terms sparingly and in the characters' context to attempt to give a historically accurate picture of the times.

Tanya Landman

Our books are tested
for children and young people by
children and young people.

Thanks to everyone who consulted on
a manuscript for their time and effort in
helping us to make our books better
for our readers.